A DORLING KINDERSLEY BOOK

Photography by Philip Dowell
Additional Photography by Michael Dunning
(pages 10-11 and 14-17)
Illustrations by Martine Blaney,
Dave Hopkins, and Colin Woolf

Text copyright and photographs
(pages 4-5, 10-11, and 14-17) copyright © 1991
by Dorling Kindersley Limited, London
Photographs (pages 6-9, 12-13, and 18-21)
copyright © 1991 by Philip Dowell

Aladdin Books
Macmillan Publishing Company
866 Third Avenue
New York, NY 10022

First published in Great Britain in 1991
by Dorling Kindersley Limited,
9 Henrietta Street, London WC2E 8PS

Reproduced by Colourscan, Singapore
Printed and bound in Italy by L.E.G.O., Vicenza

1 2 3 4 5 6 7 8 9 10

ISBN 0-689-71403-3
Library of Congress CIP data is available.

·EYE·OPENERS·

Farm Animals

ALADDIN BOOKS
MACMILLAN PUBLISHING COMPANY
NEW YORK

Cow

horns

mouth

Farmers milk their cows every day, so that we have fresh milk to drink. A baby cow is called a calf. A calf sucks milk from its mother's udder. Cows live out in the fields. They eat a lot of grass.

cow

calf

Sheep

A mother sheep is called an ewe. An ewe has her lambs in the springtime. In early summer farmers shear their sheep. The winter fleece is spun into wool.

ewe

8

mouth

tail

lamb

9

Chicken

A mother hen lays her eggs and sits on them to keep them warm. Fluffy yellow chicks hatch from the eggs after three weeks. The hen teaches her chicks to peck the ground to look for food.

beak

chick

hen

11

Pig

A mother pig is called a sow. She has about 14 piglets at a time. Some pigs live indoors in a pigsty. Others are kept outdoors. When it's hot, they lie down in wet mud to keep cool.

snout

sow

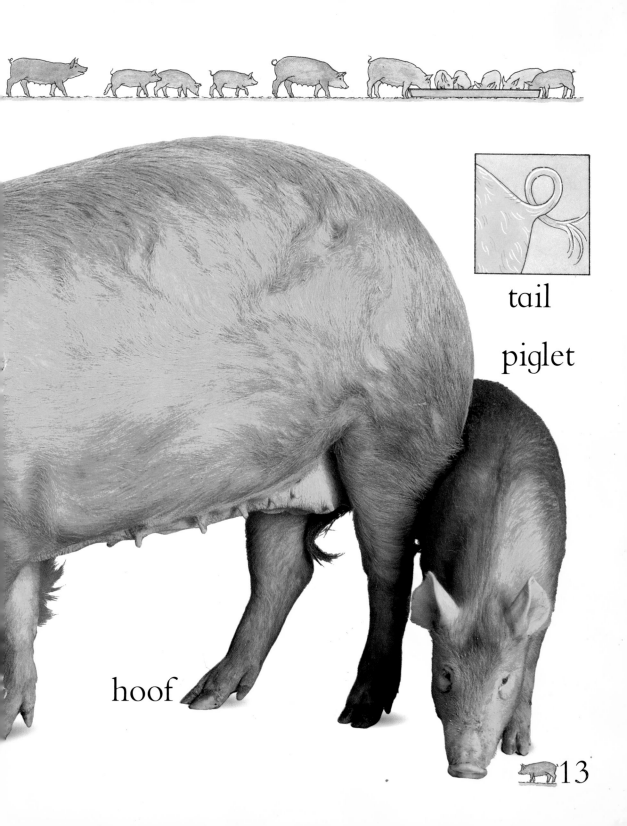

tail

piglet

hoof

13

Horse

Some farmers keep work horses to pull heavy carts and machinery. Other farmers have horses for riding. A horse wears metal shoes to protect its hooves. A blacksmith nails on the shoes, but it does not hurt the horse.

mouth

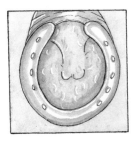

hoof

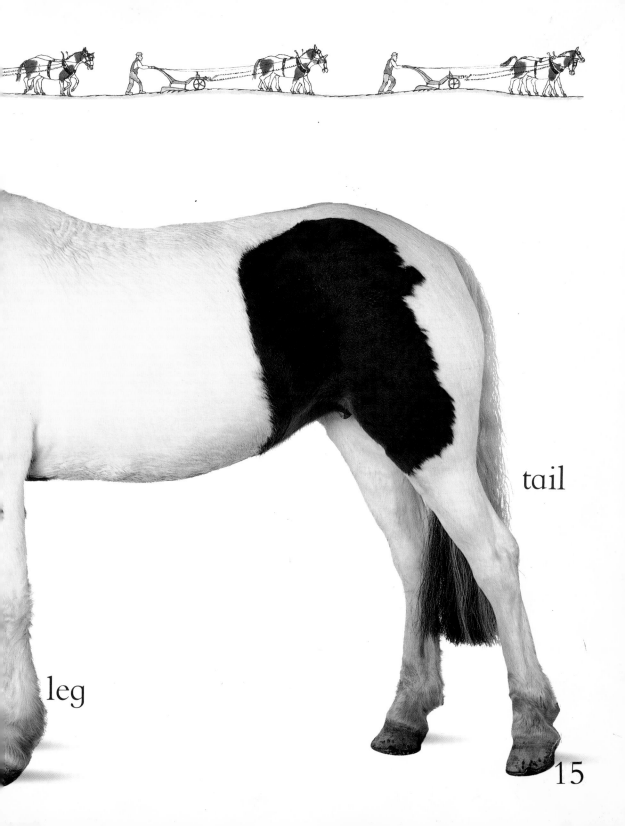

tail

leg

15

Duck

Ducks usually live near the barnyard pond or stream. They search for food in the water. Ducks eat worms, waterweeds, and seeds.

A young duck is called a duckling.

ducklings

duck

foot

beak

tail

Goat

A mother goat is called a
nanny goat. Farmers milk
their nanny goats. The
milk is usually turned into
cheese. Young goats are
called kids. Kids playfully
butt and chase each
other around the fields.

nanny goat

beard

mouth

kid

udder

19

Farm dog

Farm dogs work hard for the farmer. They help round up sheep and other animals into pens. The dogs are trained to obey the farmer's calls and whistles.

ear

tail

muzzle

paw

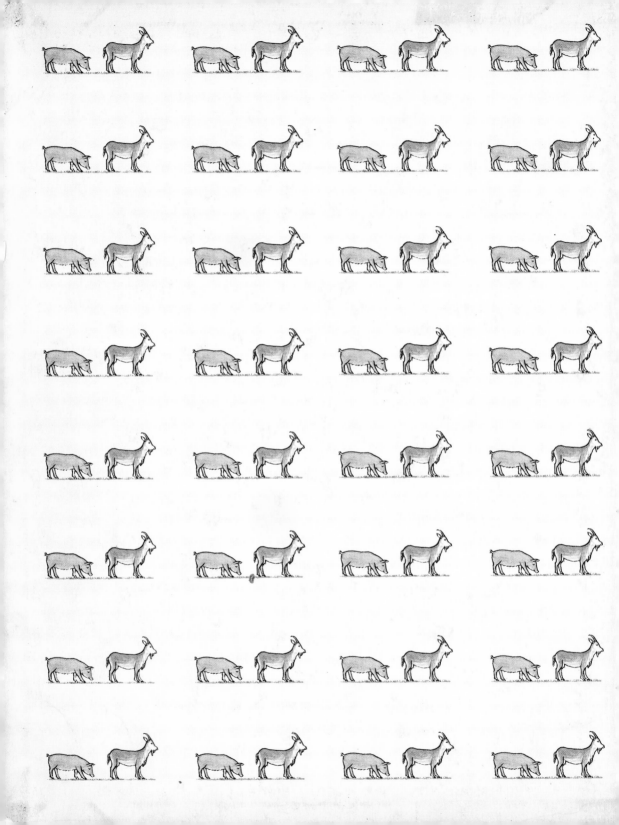